Contents

Illustrated by Vince Reid

First Published 2010 in Great Britain by

A CIP record for this work is available from the British Library

ISBN-10: 1-905637-92-6
ISBN-13: 978-1-905637-92-8

Typeset by Educational Printing Services Limited

Educational Printing Services Limited
Unit 6, Glenfield Park 2, Northrop Avenue, Blackburn BB1 5QH
Telephone: (01254) 686500   Fax: (01254) 686501
E-mail: enquiries@eprint.co.uk   Website: www.eprint.co.uk

Jack O' Lantern

Jack was drunk. He was staggering home from the pub with a kebab in one hand and trying to steady himself with the other. After a while he came to the local graveyard; he leaned on the wall with one hand and munched on his kebab with the other.

Just then, a swirling white mist rose up from one of the graves and began to take shape in the air. The mist became a white ghostly figure that whispered, **"Woo . . . Woooooo . . . Woooooooooo!"**

"Alright there, mate!" said Jack. "How are you tonight then? Erm . . . would you like a bit of kebab?"

"Jack . . . Jack . . . Jack!" boomed the ghost. **"You are the first person to speak to me in three hundred and forty seven years. For that reason, I will grant you three wishes."**

"Three wishes!" exclaimed Jack. "What

will I wish for? Erm, I know! My wife is always sending me off for firewood and every time I fill up my sack, I always trip over and drop the wood all over the floor. I wish that whatever I put in my sack has to stay in there until I give it permission to get out."

"That's a strange wish," mused the ghost, **"what else do you wish for?"**

"Erm, what next? Oh! I know! I have

2

a lovely apple tree in my garden but every time the fruit is ripe and I go to pick an apple, they're gone! The children in my village are always stealing them. Scrumping my apples, that's what they do! I wish that whoever grabs one of my apples won't be able to let go unless I give permission!"

"Hmmm, strange indeed," said the ghost, **"but have it your way. What is your final wish?"**

"Erm, alright then. What else bothers me now? Ah! My wife is always inviting people into our house. Every time I get in from the pub or from gathering wood there's always someone sitting in my armchair! I wish that whoever sits in my armchair won't be able to get up unless I give them permission!"

"You're a very strange man, Jack," said the ghost and then disappeared into a white mist once more.

Jack staggered home, then collapsed onto the sofa fast asleep.

In the morning he woke up, peeled the kebab from his cheek and his wife sent him out for firewood.

While collecting the wood he suddenly

screamed,

"OWWWWWWWWWWW!!! I've got a splinter in my finger! OWWWW!!! Oh dear Lord it hurts!"

Jack ran home and showed his wife the splinter. He writhed on the floor in pain. His wife got a needle and tried to get the splinter out but, "OOOOOOOOOOOWWWWWWW WWWW!!!" Jack screeched. "You've made it even worse now! You pushed it right under the nail! Oh, I'd give anything to take away the pain!"

As Jack said those words there was a KNOCK! KNOCK! KNOCK! at the door.

Jack's wife answered it and there stood a man. A man with goat's legs. A man carrying a pitchfork. A man with a goatee beard. A man with two horns sticking out of his forehead.

"Hello," said the Devil, "I'm here to see the sick man."

"Oh!" Jack's wife said. "How did you know there was a sick man? Come in! He's in the living room."

"Hello, Jack," smiled the Devil, "would you like me to take away the pain?"

"OH! Yes please! I'd give you anything

4

to take away the pain! You can have my house! You can have my cow! You can have my wife! Anything!"

"I don't want your house, or your cow or your wife," the Devil hissed, "I want your *soul*!"

"You can have it! You can have it! Just take away the pain!" screamed Jack.

The Devil slammed the pitchfork into the ground and the pain instantly disappeared.

"I'll be back for you in seven years," smiled the Devil, "ta-ta!"

The Devil then walked out of the house.

Jack and his wife lived happily for seven years, but eventually there came a KNOCK! KNOCK! KNOCK! at the door.

Jack answered it and there stood the Devil.

"Are you ready to come with me?" asked the Devil.

"I just need a moment to say goodbye to the wife," said Jack glumly. "Would you like to come in and have a seat by the fire?"

"Thank you, I will," the Devil said as he sat in Jack's armchair.

Jack put on his coat, said goodbye to his wife and said, "Come on, then."

The Devil tried to get up but found that he was stuck in the armchair!

"What's going on here?!" bellowed the Devil. "Why can't I get out of this chair?"

The Devil pulled and pushed, heaved and hauled, but no matter what he did he just couldn't get out of that armchair!

"You'll not be able to get out unless I give you permission," laughed Jack, "and I'll not do that unless you give me another seven years."

"WHAT?!" boomed the Devil. "Not a chance!"

"Alright then, I'm off out. See you later!"

"NO!" the Devil screeched. "I don't want to sit here. What if the fire goes out? I'll be cold! Alright Jack, you've got seven years; but then I'll be back!"

The Devil stormed out of the house in a terrible rage after Jack had given him permission to get out of the armchair.

Jack and his wife lived happily for another seven years, but then there came another

KNOCK! KNOCK! KNOCK! at the door.

Jack answered it and there stood the Devil.

"Are you ready to come with me this time?" asked the Devil angrily.

"Would you not like a sit down before we go?" Jack said.

"NOOO!" thundered the Devil.

"Alright," said Jack sadly, "let's go."

Jack put on his coat, said goodbye to his wife and both he and the Devil walked through his back garden.

Just then Jack said, "Have you seen my apple tree. Isn't that the nicest apple tree you've ever seen?"

"Yes, it's very nice. I'm quite fond of apples myself," said the Devil.

"Would you just get me one apple for the journey . . . please?"

"Oh, alright," said the Devil as he reached over and grabbed an apple. But as he tried to pull it from the tree the Devil found that he was stuck to the apple

"What's going on here?" demanded the Devil. "Why can't I let go of this apple?"

"You'll not be able to let go unless I give you permission," laughed Jack again, "and I'll not do that unless you give me another seven years."

"W – WHAT?!" spluttered the Devil. "No way; not this time!"

"Alright then, I'm going to the pub. I hear it's going to be a *cold* night! See you later!"

"NO!" the Devil screamed. "I don't want to be stuck here! Alright, Jack, you've got another seven years; but then I'll be back!"

Jack released the Devil and watched as he fumed out of the back gate in a terrible rage.

Jack and his wife lived happily for yet another seven years, but once again there was a KNOCK! KNOCK! KNOCK! at the door. Jack answered it and there stood the Devil.

"No tricks," said the Devil. "Let's go."

Jack put on his coat, said goodbye to his wife and he and the Devil walked through the back garden.

"Would you not like an apple for the journey?" asked Jack.

"I don't want any of your wretched fruit!" screamed the Devil.

"Fair enough," said Jack.

They walked along a muddy track in silence until Jack said, "Oh! I know where we are! This is where I used to play as a child! We used to play 'jump in the sack'!"

"'Jump in the sack'? What's that?" asked the Devil.

"It's easy!" said Jack pulling his sack from his coat pocket and placing it on the ground. "You go . . . into the sack and out of

the sack, into the sack and out of the sack, into the sack and out of the sack, like that."

The Devil watched Jack jumping in and out of the sack and said, "That's the stupidest game I've ever seen!"

"It's only because you can't do it!" challenged Jack.

"Nonsense," scoffed the Devil, "stand back and watch this!"

The Devil leapt into the sack but found that he was stuck! He couldn't get back out!

"What's going on here!?" demanded the Devil. "Why can't I get out of this sack?"

"You'll not be able to get out unless I give you permission," laughed Jack, "and I'll not do that unless you give me another seven years."

"NEVER!" screamed the Devil. "Not a chance! Not this time."

"Alright then," said Jack and he pulled the sack up and over the Devil's head, tied a knot and shouted, "who wants a game of footie?!"

Everyone ran from their houses and into the street.

"Where's the ball?" someone asked.

"I haven't got one!" beamed Jack.

"We'll just have to use this sack!"

The football match went on for a full ninety minutes with over thirty players kicking the sack up and down the street.

At the end of the ninety minutes no-one had scored. So they played a further thirty minutes extra time.

Then there were penalties; five each.

"Alright," came a whimpering voice from the sack, "you can have your seven years, just stop kicking me!!!"

Jack opened the sack and poured the Devil onto the ground. The Devil literally pulled himself together and staggered off.

Jack invited everyone back to his house for a party. There was drinking and dancing and there, in the middle of it all, Jack had a heart attack and collapsed dead on the floor.

Jack's spirit went drifting up, up, up to Heaven.

At the pearly gates he met St Peter himself.

"Hello!" said Jack cheerfully. "Can I come in, please?"

"I'm afraid not, Jack," answered St Peter. "You have been making deals with the

Devil. It's downstairs for you."

So Jack's spirit went drifting down, down, down to Hell.

At the gates of Hell, Jack knocked and waited.

A little demon opened a slat in the gate and screeched, "What do you want?!"

"Hello," said Jack, less cheerfully. "Can I come in please?"

"Just a minute and I'll check!" the demon squeaked then went off to find the Devil.

"It's Jack from Ireland," the demon said once he'd found the Devil, "can he come in?"

"NOOO!" boomed the Devil. "Tell him to go away! Go away!!!"

The demon went back and screeched, "We don't want you; go away!" and slammed the slat shut in the gate loudly.

Jack's spirit went floating back up to Ireland where he drifted here and there, from place to place in the dark.

St Peter saw Jack and, feeling sorry for him, came down from Heaven and gave Jack a little light to guide his way.

From that day on, Jack lit paths for travellers and helped drunks find their way home.

Some people call this light 'Will-o'-the-wisp'. The next time you walk around late at night; keep looking for the light of 'Jack O' Lantern'.

Baba Yaga Bony Legs

Masha lived with her father and stepmother in a small cottage near a forest. Whenever Masha's father was around, her stepmother was good and kind to her. But once her father was out the stepmother was cruel and wicked. She treated Masha like a slave and if Masha didn't do as she was told the stepmother would threaten to beat her with a stick.

One day Masha's father was out visiting a sick friend when her stepmother said, "Go visit my sister. She lives in the middle of the forest. Ask her to lend you a needle and thread."

"But we have many needles and lots of thread in our cottage right here!" said Masha.

"Don't argue with me or I'll hit you with my stick!" screamed the stepmother.

So Masha packed herself some lunch in a red handkerchief. She put in some bread, a chicken leg and some cheese, then she set off.

After walking for a long time she grew tired so she sat down on a felled tree and unwrapped her handkerchief.

Just then, a mouse came scampering up to Masha. She couldn't help noticing how skinny the mouse looked, so she broke the bread into crumbs and sprinkled them onto the ground.

The mouse devoured them quickly, looked up at Masha and squeaked, "Oh, thank you! I was so hungry! But tell me, why are you out in the middle of this forest all alone? Don't you know that there are bears and wolves and, worst of all, a Baba Yaga lives in this forest!"

"My stepmother is sending me to see her sister who lives in the middle of the forest to borrow a needle and thread," explained Masha.

"Oh no!" squealed the mouse. "She is sending you to Baba Yaga Bony Legs! She'll eat you up! But . . . you are good and kind. If you listen to your heart; you'll be fine."

With that, the mouse scurried off into the forest.

Masha didn't feel like eating after hearing what the mouse had said, so she tied

up her lunch in the red handkerchief and
carried on with her journey.

She eventually came to a white fence
surrounding a house. As she drew nearer she
realised the fence was made of bones and the
house was standing on top of a pair of giant
chicken's legs.

The house danced from one foot to the other and seemed to be looking at Masha.

She put a hand on the gate and the house stopped moving.

She opened the gate with a CCCRRREEEAAAKKKK!

Masha stepped into the garden and a huge, fierce dog leapt at her. She quickly unwrapped the red handkerchief and threw the dog the chicken leg. The dog munched away at the leg and Masha carefully stepped past it.

She then knocked at the door and a hoarse, gruff voice croaked, *"Who is it?"*

"It's me, Masha. Your sister has sent me to you to borrow a needle and thread."

"Ooh! I know what that means! Come in!" the voice said.

Masha opened the door and there she saw Baba Yaga Bony Legs. She was hideous! She had gnarled, bony arms and legs. She had a long, crooked nose covered with warts. She had big, bushy hair that sprouted out all over her head. Her hair was infested with head lice that wriggled and jiggled all over and made it look like it was moving.

Masha saw that she had iron teeth

inside her mouth as she smiled. *"Hello! Do you know how to weave? Can you use a weaving loom?"* Baba Yaga Bony Legs asked.

"Yes I can weave," replied Masha.

"Well you sit here and get weaving while I go for a bath in the bathhouse outside. I'll know that you're still here because I'll be able to hear the CLICK – CLACK of the weaving loom. When I come back I'm going to eat my supper! Sluuurp!"

Baba Yaga left the house and Masha began weaving at the loom making a CLICK – CLACK sound.

Just then a cat walked by and sat down to watch Masha. Masha couldn't help noticing how skinny the cat looked so she took out the red handkerchief and threw the cat the cheese.

The cat leapt upon the cheese and devoured it hungrily. When it had finished the cat began washing itself.

"Oh, thank you Masha," said the cat. "But why are you still here? Don't you know that when Baba Yaga Bony Legs gets back from the bathhouse she'll eat you up?"

"But how can I leave?" asked Masha desperately. "If I stop weaving Baba Yaga

Bony Legs will know that I've gone and she'll come after me!"

"I'll weave for you," said the cat, "and if Baba Yaga Bony Legs does come after you then throw down this hand mirror. If she still comes after you then throw down this brown comb."

Masha took the mirror and the comb and thanked the cat. Then she noticed a bottle of oil on a table so she took that, too.

The cat sat at the weaving loom making a CLICK – CLACK sound and Masha crept out of the house.

Once in the garden she patted the dog on the head who was still munching on the chicken bone she had given him.

She then put the oil on the hinges of the gate. Now it opened silently and Masha ran off into the forest.

Suddenly, the trees grabbed hold of Masha. They wrapped their branches around her body and legs and neck. Masha quickly took the red handkerchief from her pocket and tied a pretty bow onto the branches of a tree. The trees let go and Masha ran as fast as she could.

Meanwhile, Baba Yaga Bony Legs had

finished her bath and walked into her house.
There she saw the cat at the weaving loom.

"*CAT!*" she screamed. *"Why are you weaving? Why didn't you scratch the girl's eyes out to stop her from leaving?"*

"Because she gave me something to eat," answered the cat, "and you've never fed me in forty years."

Then, Baba Yaga Bony Legs stormed out of the house and saw the dog eating the chicken bone.

"DOG!" she screamed. *"Why are you eating? Why didn't you bite the girl's legs to stop her from leaving?"*

"Because she gave me something to eat," answered the dog, "and all you ever do is kick me around."

Next, Baba Yaga Bony Legs rushed to the gate.

"GATE!" she screamed. *"Why didn't you creak to warn me that she was leaving?"*

"Because she oiled my hinges," answered the gate, "and all you ever do is kick me open."

Baba Yaga Bony Legs ran out of the gate and spoke to the trees.

"TREES!" she screamed. *"You belong to me! Why didn't you grab her and stop her from leaving?"*

"Because she tied a pretty bow to our branches," whispered the trees, "and all you ever do is chop us down for firewood."

Baba Yaga Bony Legs was furious! She grabbed her broomstick and with a WHHOOOOOSSSHHH!!! set off after Masha.

Masha heard Baba Yaga Bony Legs coming and so she threw down the mirror that the cat had given her.

This immediately smashed on the ground and out came a huge, wide river. Everyone knows that witches can't cross running water, so Baba Yaga Bony Legs leapt from her broomstick, got on all fours and drank up the river.

Then she was off again with a WHHOOOOOSSSHHH!!!

Masha heard Baba Yaga Bony Legs coming once more so she threw down the brown comb.

This immediately turned into a gigantic, dense forest of beech trees that grew so close together that nothing could fit in between them.

Baba Yaga Bony Legs leapt from her broomstick and with her iron teeth began biting her way through the forest.

But after drinking up the river, her teeth had gone rusty so they crumbled and fell from her mouth. She screamed and had to go back to her house hungry.

Masha ran home and told her father everything. Her father searched for the stepmother in a terrible rage, but she had gone.

Some say that she went off into the forest and got eaten by a bear. Some say that she got eaten by a wolf. But most think that she became a Baba Yaga herself and can still be heard cackling in the dark of the night.

The Breath of the Demon

There was once a Princess whose beauty was only matched by her intelligence. She was loved by all who met her . . . and those who had simply heard of her.

Word of this Princess made its way deep below the Earth. Deep into the bowels of Hell. The demons that dwelled there heard of her loveliness and they wanted to kidnap her. They wanted to keep her there; she was not to be wasted on humans!

So it was decided that one of them should get her. Get her and drag her to Hell!

But who?

Who among them would be able to complete such a task?

The demons smiled.

They knew.

The demon with the breath of Hell!

It climbed up, up, up and onto the Earth. It spread its huge, bat-like wings and took to the sky. It flew faster than any bird, higher than any cloud. It sped to the palace home of the Princess and circled the tallest tower.

The Princess was sitting reading a book by the window ledge and didn't notice the red creature flying around and around past her window. The creature then grinned a tooth-filled grin.

The demon gripped the wall of the tower beneath the window ledge with its razor-sharp claws and then it began to breathe in.

The Princess was sucked up into the demon's breath and out of the tower. She found herself sitting on its purple tongue, jailed with long, sword-like teeth blocking her escape from its mouth.

The demon took to the sky once more with the Princess screaming for help.

When the King and Queen noticed the Princess was missing they wept, wailed and whimpered; they screamed, screeched and shrieked.

But the Princess had gone.

The King and Queen offered a reward of the Princess's hand in marriage and half their kingdom to anyone who could get her back safely.

Knights travelled from far away countries to find the Princess but none could track her down.

News of her disappearance reached a blacksmith who had seven sons.

Each son was strong, honest and had a special gift.

Each one had a skill like no other.

The eldest could run faster than any living thing. The second had such hearing that he could hear grass growing on a hillside one hundred miles away. The third was so strong that he could smash down brick walls with one swing of his fist. The fourth was so sly with his hand that he could steal the eggs from a chicken without it noticing, or the glasses from your nose without *you* noticing. The fifth could stamp his foot to the ground and any kind of building would spring up from where he stamped. The sixth was such a good shot with a bow and arrow that he could split a hair on your head in two with his eyes closed. And the seventh had a voice so sweet that when he sang the dead would come back to life.

When the seven sons heard about the Princess the youngest said, "Brothers, let *us* rescue her! What use are these skills if we don't use them to do good?"

The brothers agreed and set off at once. But where would they search?

The second brother put his ear to the ground and listened.

"I hear her!" he shouted. "She is trapped below the Earth behind the gates of Hell!"

The third brother sprang into action; he began punching at the ground, pounding with his fists until at last the earth cracked open and the seven brothers fell down, down, down until they reached the gates of Hell.

The third brother pulled back his fist and smashed the iron gates wide open.

The seven brothers strode into Hell.

Each time a demon confronted them, the third brother knocked the creature flying with one punch. They found the Princess locked in an iron cage. The demon with the breath of Hell was wrapped around the cage, fast asleep and snoring.

The fourth brother sneaked his way over the demon, picked the lock and picked

up the Princess. He carried her out of the
cage, over the demon and onto the back of the
eldest brother.

The eldest brother then bolted like a
bat out of Hell with the other six brothers
running behind him. They all climbed up, up,
up and into the sunshine above.

When the demon awoke and saw the
Princess had gone he roared with fury.

The second brother heard him and
told the others, so the fifth brother stamped
his foot and made a great iron tower. The

Princess and the brothers rushed inside and locked the door just as the demon burst from the ground.

It flew through the air with ferocious speed and slammed into the iron tower. The tower shook, the tower trembled, the tower cracked at the top.

Quick as a flash the demon gripped the wall of the iron tower beneath the crack with its razor-sharp claws and began to breathe in.

The Princess was once again sucked up into the demon's breath and was trapped in its mouth.

The demon took to the sky and zoomed away with the Princess.

The sixth brother ran out of the tower, drew back his bow and let the arrow fly.

Thwack! The arrow pierced the demon through his heart and he fell to the ground . . . dead.

The eldest brother ran as swiftly as the wind to where the demon lay.

When the others caught up with him they saw that their brother wept. For the Princess had fallen below the demon. Its death meant her own. She was crushed below its huge red body.

The seven brothers rolled the demon away from her. Then all wept.

All except for the seventh brother.

He sang a song sweeter than anyone had ever heard. A song melodious and mournful.

When he had finished, the Princess sat up and said, "Have I been sleeping?"

The brothers laughed and slapped each others' backs.

The youngest of them took the Princess's hand and told her the story of her rescue.

Then the eight of them walked the long, slow walk back to her palace. As they walked, they talked, and as they talked the Princess and the youngest brother fell in love.

When they had all arrived back at the palace it was settled. The youngest brother and the Princess were to be married. The other six brothers were made wealthy. Their father was to be the proudest man that ever lived.

And so it was that they all lived happily for the rest of their days.

But . . . the demon with the breath of Hell had also been brought back to life when the youngest brother had sung.

The demon still lives today.

He is still dragging unfortunate souls to live with him in Hell.

So watch out!

A Bucket of Brains

Jack was a fool. He was always getting himself into trouble. There was the time he had tried to fish the reflection of the moon out of the river; he thought that it had fallen in! Of course the only thing that had fallen into the river that day was Jack.

Then there was the time he wondered if blue paint tasted differently to red paint. All he got was a purple mouth and a sore belly. Yes, Jack was a fool.

One day, his mother asked him to collect some water from the well.

"Where does water come from, Ma?" asked Jack.

"All things come from God," came the reply.

"But what about those lovely apples covered in toffee that we get as a treat? Don't we get those from the wise woman that lives on the hill?"

"Ah, yes," smiled his mother. "All things come from God, but if we feel the need for a nice treat, then the wise woman can get you anything you want."

Jack thought about this. Thinking was not something that came naturally to him, so this took a while.

Eventually he decided that it was brains that he needed. God hadn't given him enough brains, which was why he was a fool, so he would have to get some from the wise woman. Enough brains to make him clever like his mother. A bucket of brains!

Jack smiled to himself and set off to the top of the hill where the wise woman lived, swinging the empty bucket as he went.

He knocked at the door and waited. It was polite to wait and not to just barge into someone's house. His mother had taught him that. Even a fool knows that.

"Who is it?" came a screechy voice.

"Me," said Jack.

"Who's me?" croaked the wise woman.

"You're the wise woman," answered Jack confidently, "and I'm Jack."

The wise woman opened the door and peered at Jack deeply.

"Are you the fool from the bottom of the hill?" she asked.

"That I am!" grinned Jack.

"Come in dear, and have a cup of tea."

Jack followed the wise woman into her home and sat on a three-legged stool by the fire.

"So what is it I can do for you, my dear?" the wise woman asked.

"I need a bucket of brains!" announced Jack.

"Brains is it, my dear?"

"It is."

"Well you must bring me the heart of

the thing you love best. My cooking pot needs feeding and so do I," croaked the wise woman. "Bring me that and I'll tell you how to get your bucket of brains."

"But how do I do that? How do I know what I love best?" asked a bewildered Jack.

"It's up to *you* to find what *you* love best," smiled the wise woman with a toothless grin.

Jack set off home thinking all the way. This was the most thinking he had done his whole life and it hurt!

Just as he neared home he saw his favourite pig in the pig sty and Jack smiled.

"Of course!" he said to himself. "My pig! That's what I love best!"

Jack went and got his largest butchering knife. He killed the pig and cut out its heart. He then dropped it into the bucket and set off back up the hill.

"Who is it?" asked the wise woman when Jack knocked at her door.

"Me," answered Jack.

"Don't start that again," grumbled the wise woman as she opened the door and let Jack in.

"So, is this the heart of the thing you

love best?" asked the wise woman while smacking her lips.

"It is!" beamed Jack.

"Well, let's see then! If you can answer this question then you've got the right heart:

"Many creatures don't have one, but I have two,

"Each one is a loner but lives with four brothers,

"In a cradle, I soothe a restless child.

"What am I?"

"I – I don't know," answered Jack.

"Well then, you haven't brought me the right heart! Out you go!" said the wise woman as she pushed Jack out of the door.

Jack slowly walked home thinking all the way again. This was definitely the most thinking he had done ever and it really hurt!

Just as he neared home he decided to ask his mother what she thought was the thing he loved best of all. But Jack's neighbours were all outside his house, coming and going, this way and that.

The priest saw Jack coming and slowly stepped towards him.

"I'm sorry my child," said the priest sadly, "but your mother has passed away. She lives with God now in everlasting peace."

Jack burst into tears; he was the saddest he had ever felt in his life. Then he suddenly said, "Of course! My mother! That's what I love best!"

Jack waited until everyone had left. He looked at his mother so peaceful in her coffin. She lived with God now and wouldn't need her heart anymore. He cut it out and dropped it into the bucket.

When he got to the top of the hill he knocked and waited.

"Who is it?" came the wise woman's voice.

"Me," answered Jack.

The wise woman grumbled to herself and opened the door and let Jack in.

"So, is this the heart of the thing you love best?" asked the wise woman again.

"It is!" nodded Jack.

"Well, let's see then! If you can answer *this* question then you've got the right heart:

"I have horns but am not a beast,
"Follow my trail of silver light as
"I walk the world on my stomach,
"Never leaving my house,
"What am I?"

"I – I still don't know," answered Jack.

"Well then, you haven't brought me the right heart again, have you?! Out you go!" said the wise woman as she pushed Jack out of the door roughly.

Jack was sad. He slowly walked off home thinking some more. This was *certainly* the most thinking he had done his whole life and it *truly* hurt!

Just as he neared home he saw his neighbour's daughter, Isla, sat under the shade of a tree.

"I'm sorry to hear about your mother, Jack," Isla said.

"Me too. The funeral is tomorrow. Will you come?" he asked.

Isla came to the funeral and comforted Jack. When everyone was at his house afterwards it was Isla that made sure everyone had enough to eat and drink. It was Isla that looked after Jack in his sorrow.

When all of the mourners had left she said, "I hear that fools make the best husbands!"

In no time they were married and lived happily enough. So happily that one day Jack came home from collecting water from the

well in his bucket, when he said, "I'm going to
have to cut out your heart, Isla."

"W – What?!" Isla spluttered. "Why?"

"Because I love you best of all and I
have to take your heart to the wise woman on
top of the hill, then she'll give me a bucket of
brains."

Isla thought quickly and said, "Well if I
come with you then you'll still be taking the
heart of the thing you love best!"

"You're right!" beamed Jack and the
pair set off to the top of the hill.

"Who is it?" asked the wise woman
when Jack knocked at her door.

"Me," answered Jack.

"Oh, you again! I thought you'd given up!" grinned the wise woman as she opened the door, letting Jack and Isla in.

"So, where is the heart of the thing you love best?" asked the wise woman.

"Here it is," laughed Jack, "inside the chest of my wife!"

"Well, let's see then! If you can answer these questions then you've got the right heart:

"Many creatures don't have one, but I have two,

"Each one is a loner but lives with four brothers,

"In a cradle, I soothe a restless child.

"What am I?"

"That's easy!" answered Isla. "It's your thumbs!"

"Well then, aren't you a clever girl! Try this one;

"I have horns but am not a beast,

"Follow my trail of silver light as

"I walk the world on my stomach,

"Never leaving my house,

"What am I?"

"A snail!" beamed Isla.

"Yes!" laughed the wise woman. "And

41

here's your last one;

"You need me for sitting, although I am not a chair,

"When you are running, I am still there,

"People say I'm soft, but I'm hard to find,

"Because wherever you look, I'm always *behind*.

"What am I?"

"You're a bottom!" giggled Isla.

"Oh yes, indeed!" the wise woman roared with laughter. "It looks like you've got your bucket of brains already, Jack!"

"Have I?" asked a bemused Jack looking all around him. "But where?"

"Inside your wife's head," answered the wise woman.

Jack and Isla went home happily. Jack never wanted a bucket of brains again for he knew that his wife had enough brains for the two of them!

The Cauldron from Hell

There was once a demon in Hell.

This demon noticed that all of the people that came down to Hell from planet Earth were liars and cheats and bullies. They were thieves and vandals and murderers.

This demon wondered if everyone on planet Earth was the same.

So, he climbed up, up, up and out of Hell. He emerged through mud and dirt. The sun shone brightly on his warty green face. His black eyes winced at the sudden brightness.

Then the demon saw people coming towards him. He didn't want to be noticed so the demon immediately transformed himself into a three-legged black cauldron.

People walked past the cauldron all day long and the demon cauldron watched and listened.

Eventually, along came a poor man. When he saw the cauldron he thought to himself, "That's a fine-looking cauldron, that is. I could do with one of those to cook with . . . if I had any food! But it doesn't belong to me so I'd better leave it be, even if it is in the middle of the road."

The poor man carried on walking until he came to a rich man's house.

KNOCK, KNOCK, KNOCK, he went at the door.

The rich man opened the door and stared at the poor man, "What are you doing knocking at my door, you scruffy little man? Be gone with you!"

"W – Well," stammered the poor man, "I was hoping that I could do some work for you and in return you could give me a coin or two. Perhaps even some food. You see my wife and I are starving. We're desperate for food.

All we want to do is work and feed ourselves. Please, is there anything I can do for you?"

The rich man smiled an evil smile and said, "I'll tell you what, you can clean and dust my house from top to bottom, do the washing up, scrub the floors, cut my grass, trim my bushes and I *might* be able to help. Oh . . . AND . . . I have a few trees blocking my view of the mountain over there. I want them cut down and chopped into logs too. If you complete all of these jobs by sunset then I'll give you some money."

"Right!" exclaimed the poor man and he set to work immediately. He cleaned, dusted, washed and scrubbed inside the house. Then he cut, trimmed and chopped in the garden.

Finally, as the sun was setting, the poor man had cut down all of the trees and was half way through chopping them into logs when he had to stop. The light was fading and the blisters on his hands were bursting.

KNOCK, KNOCK, KNOCK, he went at the door of the rich man.

"Yes?" sneered the rich man.

"Well, Sir, I've done all the jobs inside your house and I've nearly finished outside. I'll come back tomorrow to finish the logs."

"No, you didn't complete everything by sunset so I'm not giving you any money," said the rich man flatly.

"What? But I've worked hard for you all day, Sir! Please give me something even if it's only a crust of bread."

"No, go away now or I'll set my dogs on you."

The poor man sadly walked away, dragging his exhausted body along the road.

Just then, he passed the three-legged cauldron; the *demon* cauldron sitting in the middle of the road.

The poor man picked it up and thought, "Maybe I'll take this home with me. It's starting to rain and it would be a shame to see this fine cauldron go rusty. If I hear of anyone missing a three-legged cauldron then I'll give it back to them."

With that the poor man carried the cauldron home. Once there, he set the cauldron onto a shelf in the kitchen then sat down at the table to tell his wife what had happened to him that day.

As he was telling his story, the poor man and his wife heard a voice say, "I'M GOING TO TRIPPLE, TRAPPLE, TROTTLE

OFF NOW."

"What was that?" they both asked together.

"ME, THE CAULDRON," came the reply, "I'M GOING TO TRIPPLE, TRAPPLE, TROTTLE OFF NOW."

"Well, where are you going to tripple, trapple, trottle off to?" asked the poor man.

"I'M GOING TO TRIPPLE, TRAPPLE, TROTTLE OFF TO THE RICH MAN'S HOUSE. SEE YOU LATER."

The cauldron suddenly leapt down from the shelf and went tripple, trapple, trottle up the road to the rich man's house.

When he got there, the cauldron went into the kitchen and began scooping up soup from the saucepan.

"I'M GOING TO TRIPPLE, TRAPPLE, TROTTLE OFF NOW."

"Oi! You can't do that!" shouted the chef. "That's the rich man's soup!"

"TOO LATE. I'M GOING TO TRIPPLE, TRAPPLE, TROTTLE OFF NOW. SEE YOU LATER."

The cauldron then went tripple, trapple, trottle all the way up the road until he got to the poor man's house.

The poor man and his wife thanked the cauldron, ate the soup, cleaned the cauldron then put him back on the shelf in the kitchen.

In the morning, the poor man and his wife were sitting by the kitchen table talking about what had happened the night before when they heard, "I'M GOING TO TRIPPLE, TRAPPLE, TROTTLE OFF NOW."

"Well, where are you going to tripple, trapple, trottle off to?" asked the poor man.

"I'M GOING TO TRIPPLE, TRAPPLE, TROTTLE OFF BACK TO THE RICH MAN'S HOUSE. SEE YOU LATER."

The cauldron suddenly leapt down from the shelf and went tripple, trapple, trottle up the road again to the rich man's house.

When he got there, the cauldron went into the living room where the butler was polishing silver forks and silver knives and silver spoons.

Quick as a flash the cauldron rushed up to the butler and scooped up all of the silver cutlery.

"I'M GOING TO TRIPPLE, TRAPPLE, TROTTLE OFF NOW."

"Hey! You can't do that!" shouted the butler. "That's the rich man's silver!"

"TOO LATE. I'M GOING TO TRIPPLE, TRAPPLE, TROTTLE OFF NOW. SEE YOU LATER."

The cauldron then went tripple, trapple, trottle all the way up the road until he got back to the poor man's house.

The poor man and his wife couldn't believe their eyes! They thanked the cauldron, then shared all of that silver with everyone in the village and put the cauldron back on the shelf in the kitchen.

The next morning, the poor man and his wife were sitting by the kitchen table talking about what had happened the day before when they heard, "I'M GOING TO TRIPPLE, TRAPPLE, TROTTLE OFF NOW."

"Well, where are you going to tripple, trapple, trottle off to?" asked the poor man.

"I'M GOING TO TRIPPLE, TRAPPLE, TROTTLE OFF BACK TO THE RICH MAN'S HOUSE."

The cauldron suddenly leapt down from the shelf and went tripple, trapple, trottle up the road once more to the rich man's house.

When he got there, the cauldron went into the rich man's bedroom where the rich man was counting out all of his golden coins. Quick as a flash the cauldron rushed up to the rich man and began scooping up all of the golden coins.

"I'M GOING TO TRIPPLE, TRAPPLE, TROTTLE OFF NOW."

"Now then, you! You can't do that!" shouted the rich man. "That's my gold!"

"TOO LATE. I'M GOING TO TRIPPLE, TRAPPLE, TROTTLE OFF NOW. SEE YOU LATER."

The rich man grabbed hold of the cauldron and pulled it towards himself, but the cauldron pulled away. So the rich man pulled again, as did the cauldron.

They began pulling and dragging, heaving and yanking, this way and that. Golden coins spilled all over the floor until suddenly the rich man *fell into* the cauldron.

"I'M GOING TO TRIPPLE, TRAPPLE, TROTTLE OFF NOW."

"Well, where are you going to tripple, trapple, trottle off to?" asked the rich man.

"I'M GOING TO TRIPPLE, TRAPPLE, TROTTLE OFF TO HELL!"

With that, the cauldron went tripple . . . trapple . . . trottle . . . and neither he nor the rich man were ever seen again.

The Monster's Mouth

Bill and Ben *loved* scary stories. Especially
stories about monsters. The scarier the better.
But the stories that frightened them the
most were the ones about the monster with
a mouth that could swallow up anything.
SLURP! You'd be sucked up in a flash. GULP!
You'd be swallowed up in one mouthful.
SWALLOW! Right down into the monster's
belly.

Whenever they went to hear the
storyteller, he would tell them stories of this
terrible monster. It made them shudder, it
made them shiver, it made them shake.

One Halloween, they listened to the
storyteller tell scary stories round a fire in the
park with their parents. When Bill and Ben
went home and to bed, they couldn't sleep.

"Do you think the stories are true?"
asked Ben.

"Course they are!" answered Bill,

who was older and knew about such things. "Everyone says so at school."

"Do you think the monster will be out tonight?" Ben said quietly.

"Probably," Bill said darkly, "it is Halloween after all. That's when *all* monsters come out."

"I'm scared," moaned Ben.

"Yeah, I know," answered Bill, then added quietly under his breath, "me too."

They finally found sleep and were dreaming of monsters when a noise woke them both.

"SSSSLUUUUURRRRRP!"

They sat up in their beds.

"SSSSLUUUUURRRRRP!"

They looked at each other.

"SSSSLUUUUURRRRRP!"

They leapt from their beds and walked slowly to the window.

"SSSSLUUUUURRRRRP!"

They opened the curtains.

"SSSSLUUUUURRRRRP!"

They looked down onto the street.

"SSSSLUUUUURRRRRP!"

They saw the monster!

"SSSSLUUUUURRRRRP!"

It stood on four short, scaly legs. Its body was as round as a hot-air balloon. Its head was also rounded but had a long, funnel-like mouth that was sucking and slurping and slobbering along the ground.

The monster rolled its yellow slitted eyes up at Bill and Ben's bedroom window.

"SSSSLUUUUURRRRRP!"

It sucked up the drain cover from the street.

"SSSSLUUUUURRRRRP!"

It sucked up a bin filled with rubbish.

"SSSSLUUUUURRRRRP!"

It sucked up lampposts, postboxes and

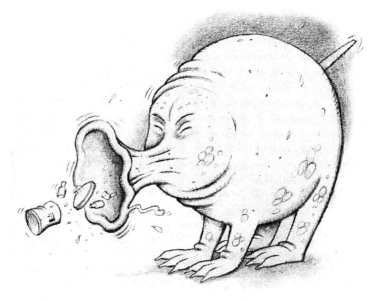

then even a cart filled with scrap!

The monster scrambled along the street sucking at anything in its path and staring at Bill and Ben.

It made it to their front door and . . .

"*SSSSLUUUUURRRRRP!*"

The door came off its hinges and into the monster's belly.

"*SSSSLUUUUURRRRRP!*"

It began racing up the stairs sucking up carpet as it went.

Bill and Ben raced into their parents' room screaming and shouting.

"Go back to bed!" their dad said angrily. "There's no such thing as monsters!"

"*SSSSLUUUUURRRRRP!*"

Mum and Dad went into the monster's belly!

Bill and Ben flew past the monster, down the stairs and into the street.

But the monster was after them.

"*SSSSLUUUUURRRRRP!*

"*SSSSLUUUUURRRRRP!*

"*SSSSLUUUUURRRRRP!*"

It chased them down roads, across pavements, along back alleys.

"*SSSSLUUUUURRRRRP!*"

Getting closer and closer. Sucking up anything in its path.

"*SSSSLUUUUURRRRRP!*"

It sucked up another drain cover in the road when suddenly it tripped. The monster's back legs fell down the drain. Then its body slipped down, too. But the monster's belly was so full of everything it had swallowed that it got stuck.

Bill and Ben stopped running; they turned and saw the monster struggling to free itself.

They looked at each other and smiled.

The boys grabbed handfuls of leaves from the wet street and crammed them into their pockets. They then ran around the monster, climbed up its back and began stuffing the wet leaves into its warty nose.

"*AAAA-CHOOOOOOOOOOOOOOO!*"

Out came the drain cover!

"*AAAA-CHOOOOOOOOOOOOOOO!*"

Out came Bill and Ben's parents!

"*AAAA-CHOOOOOOOOOOOOOOO!*"

The cart!

"*AAAA-CHOOOOOOOOOOOOOOO!*"

The lampposts!

"*AAAA-CHOOOOOOOOOOOOOOO!*

"AAAA-CHOOOOOOOOOOOOOOO!
"AAAA-CHOOOOOOOOOOOOOOO!"

The bins, the postboxes, everything it swallowed came bursting back out onto the street.

Then Bill and Ben climbed up onto its head and began leaping up and down, up and down, over and over again on the monster's squishy head. It was like leaping on a warty bouncy castle!

Eventually the monster fell down the drain where it landed with a thud.

"Hoorah!" shouted Mum and Dad.

They gave the boys a big hug and the family went back home hugging and laughing.

As for the monster? Some people think that it fell to its death. Some people think that it still lives down the drain. I don't know. But on a dark night, if you hear a *"SSSSLUUUUURRRRRP!"* noise near you, then run! Or else you might get swallowed up, too!

The White Worm

Sam was dead.

There was no denying it. He stood there looking at his bedroom all scorched and burnt.

The fire had come from the kitchen and spread all over the cottage in seconds.

Sam had lived alone so at least no one else had been hurt, but Sam still felt sad.

He had once been the joker of his village with a laugh and smile for everyone and now he was just a pile of ash. Sam sighed as he slowly walked down the stairs.

He walked right through the front door and into the morning sun. His cottage smoked and smouldered behind him as he trudged up the lane.

Neighbours and friends were running past him with buckets of water and some even ran right through him but no one saw Sam.

Round and round the village he walked until nightfall.

That was when things changed.

That was when things started to creep and crawl.

And *they* saw Sam.

There were other ghosts; Sam even recognised a few of them. But there were also creatures that crawled and crept. They slithered, slimed and sloped around Sam.

"A new one!" a voice hissed.

"He's fresh meat!" another laughed.

"You must go to the graveyard!" cackled another.

"Go and see the White Worm!"

"Let him devour you or join us!"

There was nothing else for it. Sam didn't want to see the White Worm and certainly didn't want to be *devoured* by it. But Sam also didn't want to stay with these horrible creatures either. Perhaps this White Worm would give him answers, tell him what to do next.

So off Sam went. To the graveyard.

There were more creatures.

More than Sam could have ever imagined. They flew, walked, oozed, and prowled around the gravestones.

And there, in the middle of them all sat

the White Worm.

It was enormous. The white, slimy skin glistened in the moonlight. It moved its huge head back and forth across the night sky. Then it stopped. It seemed to be sniffing the air.

It stretched itself towards Sam.

"AH, SAM," it boomed, "I SEE YOU'RE DEAD, THEN?"

"So it would seem," Sam said sadly.

"WELL IF YOU WANT TO GO OFF TO HEAVEN THEN I MUST EAT YOU UP."

"Really?!" gasped Sam. "Is there no other way?"

"DON'T WORRY, IT WON'T HURT A BIT."

"Very well, get on with it then." Sam closed his eyes.

"WELL I CAN'T EAT YOU LIKE THAT NOW, CAN I?" laughed the White Worm, "YOU MUST GO AND GET YOUR BODY."

"B – but my body was burnt."

"BLURGH! THEN YOU WON'T TASTE VERY NICE THEN, WILL YOU? BUT NEVER MIND, IT WON'T BE THE FIRST TIME I'VE HAD TO HAVE BARBECUE! HA! HA! HA!"

Sam ran straight off to his cottage and glided through the front door. His friends and neighbours had collected his ashes and taken them away, so Sam went straight off to the morgue.

There were creatures of every sort there, too.

Sam rushed past them and collected an urn that held his ashes, clearly marked with his name.

Once back at the graveyard Sam tipped

the ashes onto a flat gravestone in front of the White Worm.

The great slithering beast bent down and sniffed deeply.

"YOU AREN'T ALL HERE, SAM. I CAN'T EAT YOU LIKE THAT."

"What do you mean?" asked Sam.

"THERE ARE BITS MISSING. GO AND FIND THEM."

Sam walked off mumbling. He went back to his cottage and into his bedroom. There, he scooped up some ashes from the bed, the floor and the bedside table.

"That must be the lot!" he said to himself as he hurried back to the graveyard.

"NO," boomed the White Worm once he had inspected the rest of Sam's ashes. "THERE ARE SOME VERY SMALL PARTS MISSING."

"Like what?" asked a bewildered Sam, "I searched everywhere in my bedroom! I'm certain there's nothing left."

"HMM," pondered the White Worm, "DID YOU CUT YOUR TOENAILS BEFORE BED LAST NIGHT? JUST BEFORE YOU DIED?"

"I did! That's it!" exclaimed Sam. "But I

really don't know if I'll find those."

"FIND THEM OR I CAN'T EAT YOU."

Sam ran off once more and returned to his cottage. He searched the bin in his bedroom, the bin in the bathroom, the bin in the kitchen. He searched every floor in the house. He searched from top to bottom but he couldn't find the toenails anywhere.

After searching for hours the first light of morning came creeping through the window.

Sam didn't know why but he felt he should tell the White Worm that he wanted to be eaten before daylight. It seemed important somehow.

He raced back to the graveyard and said, "I couldn't find them anywhere; you'll just have to eat me as I am."

"SORRY, SAM. I HAVE TO EAT YOU WHOLE. IF YOU AREN'T COMPLETE THEN I CANNOT EAT YOU."

"Th – then what is to become of me?" asked Sam sadly.

"YOU ARE TO WALK THIS EARTH. WALK THIS EARTH WITH THE OTHERS THAT YOU SEE BEFORE YOU."

All of the creatures laughed as one.

It was a terrible, terrifying noise.

And the White Worm buried itself deep under the ground.

Sam still walks this Earth even today, searching for his toenails. Searching for a way to get to Heaven.

If he can't find them, then watch out; because he might decide to take yours instead!

The Cow That Ate the Piper

There was once a piper in the Highlands of Scotland. He was a traveller, he had no home. This piper, he loved his life; he loved playing the most beautiful music and in return people would give him food and shelter for the night.

But his one problem was his boots. His boots had great holes in them that would let in the rain or the snow or the mud. His feet were so sore that the piper wished above everything else that he had a new pair of boots.

One winter, the piper was walking over a hill through a swirling, whirling snowstorm. He had under one arm his pipes and under his other he had his pipe repair kit. The storm was so fierce that the piper wrapped a blanket around himself tightly, looking for a place to spend the night.

His feet were giving him terrible trouble and once more he wished he had a new pair of boots. As he made that wish he suddenly tripped over something sticking out of the snow.

The piper looked back and there he saw a brand new pair of boots! Boots made of a soft brown leather, boots with a fur lining poking out of the top.

The piper looked around and when he saw no-one coming to claim the boots, he bent down and tried to pull them out of the snow.

He pulled and dragged and heaved out of the snow . . . a dead body! A dead body frozen stiff! A dead body wearing the boots!

Well, the piper decided that this man wouldn't need these boots anymore, so he undid the laces and tried to get them off, but they were frozen solid to the man's feet.

Then the piper had an idea. He unwrapped his pipe repair kit and he took out a long, thin saw.

The piper held onto the man's leg, rested the saw just above the foot and began to saw and hack, saw and hack, saw and hack. Eventually, one foot came off. So he started on the other. Saw and hack, saw and hack, saw and hack, until the other came off, too.

Finally, the piper threw the boots with

the feet still inside over his shoulder, holding them by the laces. He gathered his pipes and his repair kit, then set off to find shelter and perhaps even somewhere to defrost his new boots.

After a while, the piper came to an old farmhouse. He put the frozen boots down near a barn, as there's nothing stranger than knocking on someone's door with a pair of feet in your hands!

The piper knocked at the door and an old woman answered.

"Who are you and what do you want?" she croaked.

"I'm a piper," he explained, "I was hoping that I could beg off you some food and shelter for the night and in return I'll play my pipes."

"Oooh!" squealed the old woman. "We like a bit of pipe music! But we haven't much room in the house; you'll have to sleep in the barn over there with the cow. Come in, come in!"

The farmer was sitting by the fire and said, "Who's this then, wife?"

"He's a piper, he's going to play us some music!"

And that's exactly what he did. The piper played all night long, the farmer and his wife had a fantastic night; they clapped and sang and danced. The piper had a grand night too; he had three bowls of broth and many glasses of whisky.

Then, at the end of the night, the piper bid the farmer and wife a good evening and set off to sleep in the barn. He collected the frozen feet on his way in. The piper noticed the cow sleeping on the straw. He went over and patted the cow, just to be polite, and as he did so, he couldn't help noticing how warm the cow felt.

"This could be an excellent place to defrost my boots!" he said to himself.

So the piper pushed the frozen boots under the cow, lay down on the straw and fell fast asleep.

In the morning, his first thought was his aching and sore feet. But he remembered his boots under the cow and went over to see if they had defrosted.

He pulled the boots out from under the cow and as he did the cow got to her feet. Sure enough, there was a pool of blood; the feet had defrosted!

So, the piper undid the laces and with a SLURGHPT! he pulled out one foot. Then with a SLURGHPT! he pulled out the other foot.

The piper took off his old boots, slipped on the new ones and they felt glorious! He felt like doing a dance and a jig right there in the middle of the barn!

But when he saw the old, mouldy feet and the worn, broken boots he wondered what he should do with them. As the piper stood there, staring at them, he had an idea; he pushed the old, mouldy feet into the worn, broken boots.

Now the piper had drunk so much the night before that he needed to go to the toilet. But he didn't want to wake the farmer and his wife, so he went round the back of the barn for his early morning wee.

Meanwhile, the farmer and his wife had woken up. The farmer's wife said, "That piper last night was brilliant! I'm going to make him his breakfast!"

She made three bowls of porridge and three mugs of tea. Then she went outside to the barn and knocked at the door. The door swung open and there she saw a pool of blood;

she saw the piper's old boots with two stumps sticking out of them . . . and she saw the cow standing above the boots, chewing away.

"AAAARRRGGGHHH!" she screamed. "The cow's eaten the piper!"

She ran to get her husband and dragged him to the barn, "The cow's eaten the piper!" she kept saying.

The farmer and his wife looked into the barn. There the farmer saw the blood and the boots and the cow.

"AAAARRRGGGHHH!!!" they both

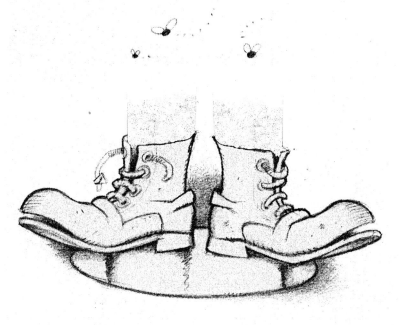

screamed as they ran off, never to be seen again.

The piper heard the scream so he came back round the barn, looked inside and when he couldn't see the farmer and his wife, the piper went to the house. He knocked at the kitchen door and the door swung open.

The piper saw the three mugs of tea and the three bowls of porridge.

"I must be getting my breakfast, too!" he said to himself.

He went inside, sat down, drank the tea and ate the porridge.

The piper waited for the farmer and his wife to come home; but they didn't. So he decided to do a few jobs on the farm, to look after the place until they did come home.

That night, he slept on the kitchen floor, then in the morning made himself some breakfast and again worked on the farm.

Two nights became three. Three nights became four. Four became a week. A week became two weeks. Two weeks became a month. A month became three months.

The piper discovered that he loved living and working on the farm! No more travelling; this was the life for him! He would stay right there until the farmer and his wife came home.

One night, when the piper was sitting with his feet up by the fire, wearing his new boots of course, there came a . . . knock . . . knock . . . knock at the door.

The piper answered it and there standing in the doorway was a man . . . a very short man . . . a *short* man with *no feet!*

"I've come for my feet," he said grimly.

"AAAARRRGGGHHH!" screamed the piper as he ran off and was never seen again either.

But what has been seen again, walking around the Highlands of Scotland, is a very short man with no feet. And if you see him – stay away – because he might be after yours!

Also available from:

PUBLISHING

Monstrous Myths: The Kings of Ancient Greece by
Adam Bushnell
ISBN 978-1-905637-84-3
King Midas . . . King Sisyphus . . . King Minos . . . These
three kings were the craziest, cleverest and cruellest of all
of the Kings of Ancient Greece. Their stories tell the tales of
Heracles, Pegasus, Icarus, the dreaded Minotaur and many
more famous mythical characters.
Suitable for 9 – 12 year olds.

**Monstrous Myths: Invade and Settle, Raid and
Meddle** by Adam Bushnell
ISBN: 978-1-905637-85-0
The Vikings and the Anglo Saxons; some of the meanest
and most menacing men that the world had ever seen. They
invaded, they settled, they raided and they meddled . . . Meet
the super hero Beowulf, the cruel King Nidud, foolish Frodi
and many others. Storyteller Adam Bushnell gives us eight
brand new retellings of classic Norse myths. A lively and
surprising collection of tales to read or to tell.

Monstrous Myths: Pyramids and Pussycats by Adam
Bushnell
ISBN: 978-1-905637-93-5
Prepare to step back into Ancient Egypt. This is a realm
of pharaohs and kings, gods and monsters, battles and
bloodshed. These stories of treachery, cunning, love and
friendship are retold in a brand new way with some serious
silliness!

Old Tales, New Twists: Snakes' Legs and Cows' Eggs
by Adam Bushnell
ISBN 978-1-905637-21-8
Selected for the SLA Boys into Books (5–11) 2008 List.

Old Tales, New Twists: Donkeys' Wings and Worms' Stings by Adam Bushnell
ISBN 978-1-905637-50-8

Old Tales, New Twists: Fishes' Claws and Dinosaurs' Paws by Adam Bushnell
ISBN 978-1-905637-76-8
What happens when you sneeze with your eyes open?
When a woodcutter meets a dragon? When a giant wants
a new slave? Or when fire monsters try to keep the world
feeling icy?

The three books in the *Old Tales, New Twists* series
include traditional tales and brand new stories, each told
with serious silliness. Each book comprises eight stories
which bring together characters from all over the world.
Suitable for 8 – 12 year olds.

Whispers in the Woods by Mark Bartholomew
ISBN 978-1-904904-61-8
Discovered lost in the woods and taken in by local
villagers, two mysterious green children find themselves
caught up in a quest to track down their missing father.
They encounter many strange and wonderful characters
but none are more terrifying than Silas of Wickham, the
witch finder who relentlessly pursues them.
Suitable for 9 year olds and above.

Chaos in the Cathedral by Mark Bartholomew
ISBN 978-1-904904-94-6
The quest of the green children continues as they search
the plague-ridden streets of Lincoln, looking for the one
man who can help them find Robin Hood, who might be
their father. The children manage to escape the clutches
of the Master of the Lincoln Gilds and leave chaos in their
wake as they flee the quarantined cathedral before it's too
late! However, in Sherwood, one of them is captured . . .
Suitable for 9 year olds and above.

Swords in the Summer by Mark Bartholomew
ISBN 978-1-905637-31-7
Leaving Sherwood Forest and Robin Hood far behind them,
Fern, Hickory and Nathaniel ride west to the ancient
Celtic land of Cornwall. Here they must find the legendary
warrior known as the Green Knight, but Cornwall is in
the midst of war and the children soon find themselves
embroiled in a bitter struggle to defend the realm against
invasion . . .
Suitable for 9 year olds and above.

Beneath the Bombers' Moon by David Webb
ISBN 978-1-900818-33-9
It is October 1940 and the air raids have begun over
Thornley. Sparky and his best friend, John, like to spend
time with Sparky's uncle in the signal box at the train
station. One day they overhear the guards discussing two
ammunition trains that have been hit. The next one will
soon be passing through Thornley . . . will Thornley be a
target? Is information being passed to the Germans? If so,
who is doing it?
Suitable for 8 – 12 year olds.

Eye of the Storm by David Webb
ISBN 978-1-900818-56-8
Danny Sharpe didn't really want to go to the City Museum in the first place. At the end of the afternoon, Danny's teacher is desperate to get his class back to school before a thunderstorm breaks out, but Danny has lost his bag. When Danny wanders into the museum's Victorian street, the storm breaks with full force, and Danny embarks on the adventure of a lifetime . . .
Suitable for 8 – 12 year olds.

Watchers of the Sky by Stephanie Baudet
ISBN 978-1-904904-43-4
Since witnessing the plane crash in which Douglas Bader lost his legs, Philip has admired the air ace as he copes with such a disability. He himself suffers from dyslexia and although no name has yet been given to it, he knows that he is not as stupid as everyone thinks. Bader's true exploits are relayed to Philip by his aircraft engineer father. Philip prepares to leave school and hold down a part-time job, as well as coping with rationing, air raids and the discovery of a German parachute . . .
Suitable for 9 –14 year olds

Moving On by Margaret Nash
ISBN 978-1-904904-42-7
Moving On is a story that takes place in the late 1950s/ early 1960s when motorbikes and pop music were 'the thing'. The story is loosely set in Liverpool amongst newly-opened Wimpy bars, Beatles' music, skyscraper buildings and the old pea-souper fogs.
Suitable for 10 –14 year olds

Order online @ **www.eprint.co.uk**